*To a wonderful family we know: Patti, Mike, the
fantastic Karly, and the real-life Claire, who as
a little girl actually said she was "full of empty."
And to all parents and children—because the
world so utterly depends on them.*

TM AND PM

For my family.

RS

Published by Familius LLC, www.familius.com

Familius books are available at special discounts for bulk purchases for sales promotions or for
family or corporate use. Special editions, including personalized covers, excerpts of existing books,
or books with corporate logos, can be created in large quantities for special needs. For more
information, contact Premium Sales at 559-876-2170 or email specialmarkets@familius.com.

Library of Congress Cataloging-in-Publication Data

2015955957
ISBN 9781942934356

Cover and book design by David Miles
Edited by Laurie Deursch

10 9 8 7 6 5 4 3 2 1

First Edition

FULL OF EMPTY

TIM J. AND M. P. MYERS

ILLUSTRATIONS BY

REBECCA SORGE

omething was wrong with Princess Claire. Her smile had flown away like a bird.

laire lived in a big, busy castle where everyone always had lots to do. On this particular day, as they all rushed about doing important things, she sat alone on the drawbridge looking gloomy. And it wasn't the first time she'd felt that way. But this time the page boy noticed her and ran to tell her mother and father.

The king and queen came rushing out.

"Angel!" said her mother. "Whatever is wrong?"

"Darling!" said her father. "Your smile has flown away like a bird!"

Claire frowned. "I don't know. I'm just . . . full of empty."

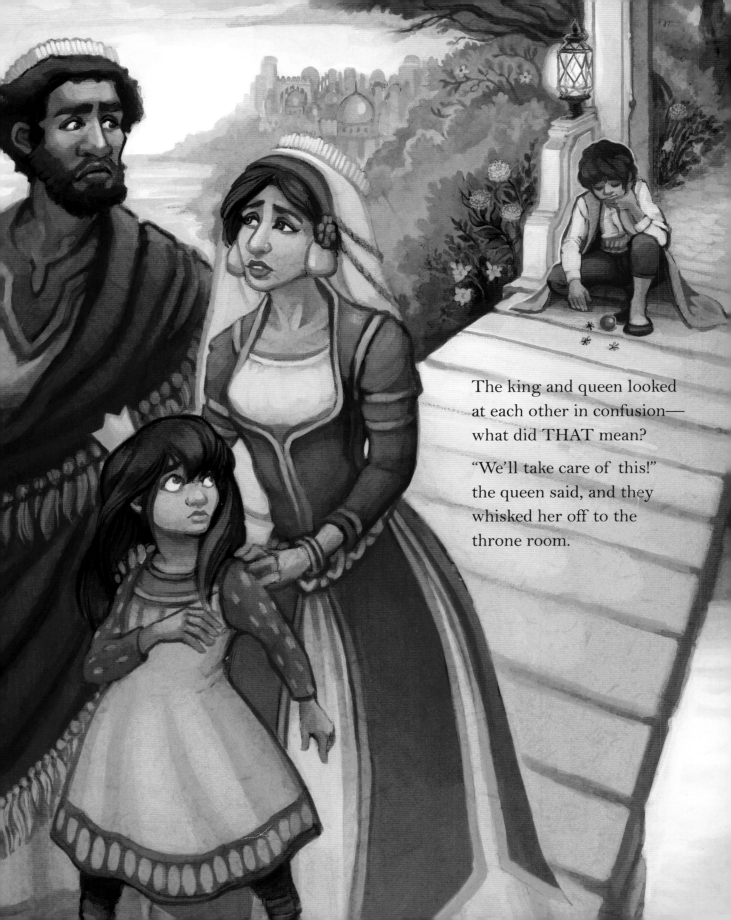

The king and queen looked at each other in confusion— what did THAT mean?

"We'll take care of this!" the queen said, and they whisked her off to the throne room.

irst, they called the doctor, and he looked Claire over from top to toesies—but she was perfectly healthy.

So what was wrong with Princess Claire?

 hen they called the royal cook and in he came, his helpers carrying trays heaped with shimmering fruits and delicious pastries, stews and roasts and eggs and vegetables, cookies and breads—all her favorite dishes. There was even a fluffy pink cake shaped like a pig, her favorite animal.

"Thank you," Claire said, "but I'm not hungry. I'm just . . . full of empty."

So what was wrong with Princess Claire?

he minister of entertainment stepped forth and called the royal entertainers—jugglers and actors and dancers and puppeteers and acrobats and a dozen more besides. "Now, Princess!" said the minister. "Who shall perform first?"

"Thanks," Claire said politely, "but I don't feel like watching anything. I'm just . . . full of empty."

So what was wrong with Princess Claire?

**T**hen they called the royal storyteller. "What story would you like?" he asked. "Dragons? Mermaids? Flying horses? Flying horses that fall in love with dragons disguised as mermaids?"

"That's nice," Claire said, "but I don't feel like a story right now. I'm just . . . full of empty."

So what was wrong with Princess Claire?

he minister of music stepped forward. She called her musicians and singers and in they came, singing heartily and playing their splendid instruments. The music soared and swelled and everyone felt lighter and happier. But Claire was still frowning.

"I'm sorry," she said, "but I don't feel like music today. I'm just . . . full of empty."

So what was wrong with Princess Claire?

hen they called the royal toymakers. "What shall we make?" they called out cheerily. "Stuffed animals or books or dolls or games or ships or skates or . . ."

"No," Claire sighed, "but thank you. I'm just . . . full of empty."

She didn't want toys?

Not even TOYS?!

No one could think of anything else. They all
looked at the king and queen.

ell," the king announced, "there's work to do—let's get back to it!"
Everyone left the throne room to tend to their duties.

"But what about Claire?" the queen asked.

"I don't know!" the king said sadly. He looked around. "Where IS Claire? She was here a minute ago!"

Suddenly, the page boy was standing next to them. "I know where she is," he whispered.

*H*e led them to the small space behind the thrones. There sat Claire, frowning as she leaned against the long purple curtains.

 aybe you should sit on the floor by her," the page whispered. The king and the queen sat. Then the page took something out of his pocket: jacks and a ball. He handed them to the queen.

Claire looked at the jacks, then at her mother and father—and her eyes got big. "Will you . . . play with me?" she asked. "You're not too busy?"

The king looked at the queen, and the queen looked at the king— and their eyes grew wet. Now they understood.

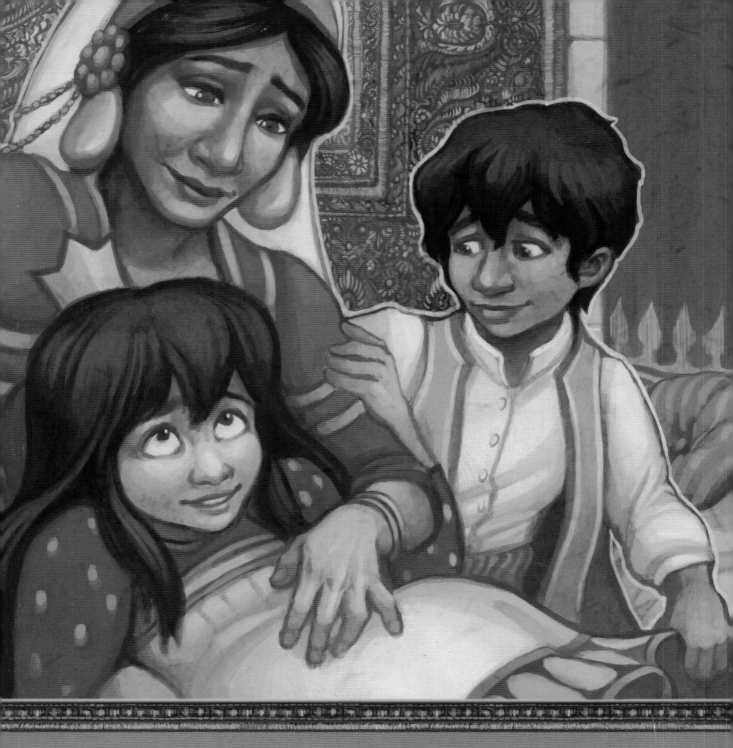

"Of course," said the queen, "but only if the page plays too."

So the four of them played together. The king accidentally sat on a jack and yelped—but everyone just laughed, including him. Then he looked serious for a moment and said, "We must play together every day."

Claire's smile came flying back like a bird.

And she made it all the way to sevensies.